For my lovely brothers
~ J.B.

LITTLE TIGER PRESS
An imprint of Magi Publications
1 The Coda Centre, 189 Munster Road,
London SW6 6AW
www.littletigerpress.com
First published in Great Britain 2002
Text and Illustrations © 2002 Jo Brown
Jo Brown has asserted her rights to be identified
as the author and illustrator of this work under
the Copyright, Designs and Patents Act, 1988.
Printed in Belgium
All rights reserved • ISBN 1 85430 783 5
1 3 5 7 9 10 8 6 4 2

Jo Brown

Where's my Mummy?

LITTLE TIGER PRESS
London

One day, a large egg
rolled out of a nest,
down a hill, and landed
at the bottom with a
CRACK!

With a push and a shove,
a small green head popped out.
It was a baby crocodile.
"Where's my mummy?" he asked.

Little Crocodile looked around and saw a monkey hanging from a branch.

"Are you my mummy?" he asked.

"Well, can you swing from a tree like me?" asked the monkey.

Little Crocodile couldn't even reach the lowest branch. "And can you do this?" said the monkey . . .

EEEE AAA

Little Crocodile tried,
but all that came out
of his mouth was . . .

Snap

"No, you're definitely
not a monkey, but I'm sure
you'll find your mummy soon."
So Little Crocodile wandered off
along the path, until he met . . .

an elephant splashing around in the water.

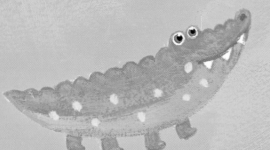

"Hello, are you my mummy?"
asked Little Crocodile.

ble u

UUUU

Snap

Little Crocodile tried, but all that came out of his mouth was . . .

"Well, you're definitely not an elephant. Keep looking for your mummy."

So Little Crocodile wandered through the forest until he met . . .

a tiger lazing in the sun.
"Hello there, are you my mummy?"
asked Little Crocodile, politely.

"Well, can you roll around in the grass like me?" asked the tiger.

"Yes!" said Little Crocodile, but he kept getting stuck . . . upside down.

"And can you do this?" asked the tiger . . .

R o

OOOARR

Little Crocodile tried, but all
that came out of his mouth was . . . Snap

The tiger definitely wasn't his mummy.

So Little Crocodile plodded
on until he came across . . .

a zebra munching some grass.

"Are you my mummy?" asked Little Crocodile, hopefully.

"Well, can you kick your back legs high up in the air like me?" replied the zebra. Little Crocodile tried but it was no use.

"And can you do this?" . . .

AYYY HEY HEY

Little Crocodile tried,
but all that came out
of his mouth was . . . **Snap**

"No, you're definitely not a zebra,
but don't be upset. I will help you
find your mummy. Hop on my back!"

And off they went.

Before long, they
arrived at the river
where Little Crocodile
saw . . .

lots of
splashing . . .

"I think I can do that!" said Little Crocodile, smiling . . .

and he could!
"And can you do this?" asked the
other crocodiles . . .

. . . as they dived in the water with their tails in the air.

"Sure," said Little Crocodile.
"And can you do this?" . . .

Snap

Snap

Snap

SNAP

Snap

Snap

YES HE COULD! Snap

"Oh, there you are!" said Mummy Crocodile,
"I've been looking for you everywhere."
She gave him a big smile.
"Where have you been?"
"Oh, just making a few friends," said
Little Crocodile.